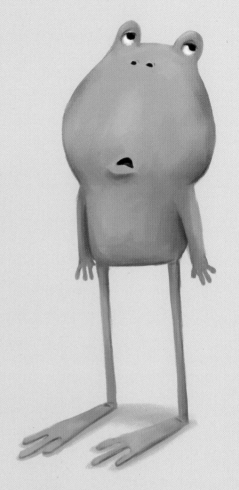

For Clio and Isla, my amazing doers.
Anyone seen the glue gun?
—Mom

To Eli, Naomi, and Alyse
on summer vacation
—Dad

THERE'S NOTHING TO DO!

written by
Dev Petty

DOUBLEDAY BOOKS FOR YOUNG READERS

illustrated by
Mike Boldt

CONTINUED
...1. Build model of Eiffel Tower.
2. Hum for three hours without stopping once.
3. Stare at the wall.
4. Try not to think about Squirrels.
(or their

What's the matter?
The day is almost over and I didn't do anything.

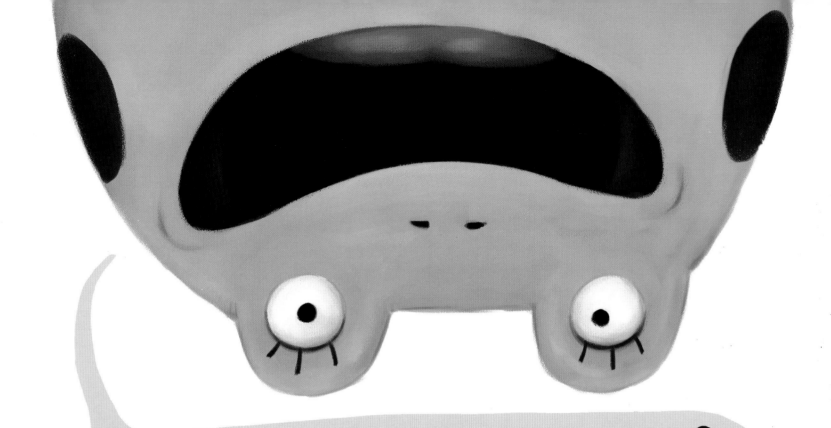

Why do you have to do anything? Just be. Watch clouds go by. Think about stuff. Then put **DO NOTHING** on your to-do list, and check it off. Sometimes the best ideas come when you stop looking for them.

Really?

Let's try it....